ANDY SHANE

and the
Know-It-All

4 books in 1

ANDY SHANE

and the

Know-It-All

4 books in 1

CANDLEWICK PRESS

CONTENTS

ANDY
SHANE
and the
Very Bossy
Dolores Starbuckle

CONTENTS

1
I Hate School

Andy Shane did not want to be in school. He did not want to be at morning meeting. He did not want to sit up straight on the rug.

He flopped down on his belly
and watched an ant carry a cracker
crumb across the floor. The ant
reminded Andy of his Granny Webb.

Granny Webb loved to catch bugs and hold them up to the sunlight. Andy wished that he were at home catching bugs with her right now.

"Ms. Janice," said a voice like a squeaky fiddle. "Ms. Janice, someone is not sitting properly!"

Andy Shane sat up quick. He knew that voice. But Andy's teacher didn't seem to hear it — even though the voice was loud, even though the voice was sitting right in front of her, even though the voice belonged to Dolores Starbuckle.

"This morning," said Ms. Janice, "we're going to find rhyming words. Can anyone tell me two words that rhyme?"

Andy Shane thought of two words: *bug* and *rug*. He looked up. Should he raise his hand?

Other kids were raising their hands. Dolores Starbuckle jumped up and down on her knees and waved her arms like a willow tree in a windstorm. Ms. Janice motioned for Dolores to sit back down.

"Andy," said Ms. Janice. She looked right at him. "Do you know two words that rhyme?"

Andy Shane opened his mouth to tell Ms. Janice the words, but they were stuck in his throat like fruit flies caught in maple syrup.

Ms. Janice waited. The other children waited, too.

"I know two words," called out Dolores Starbuckle. Andy looked at Dolores. "I know two words!" she

yelled. And before Ms. Janice could

call on her, Dolores shouted,

"*Hullabaloo* and *Kalamazoo*!"

Ms. Janice looked surprised.

She smiled. "Yes, Dolores," said

Ms. Janice. "Those words *do* rhyme."

I hate school, thought Andy Shane.

After morning meeting, Andy Shane

looked at a chart on the wall. It was

his turn to go to the math center.

Andy liked the math center. He liked

playing with the fraction puzzles and

the pattern blocks. He liked solving

the tough problems that Ms. Janice

placed there each day. But this morning, Andy wished that he could go to any other center. Yumi was in the math center. Peter was in the math center. And so was Dolores Starbuckle.

Andy Shane decided to work by himself. He would solve a problem with pattern blocks. He tried to pull

out the block bin, but it was stuck

on the math shelf. Andy Shane

pulled harder and then harder still.

The container sprang free, but all

the blocks went flying into the air.

"MS. JANICE," yelled Dolores
Starbuckle. "SOMEONE
IS MISUSING THE MATH
MATERIALS!"

2
Being Stubborn

"I don't want to go to school," said Andy Shane.

"Why not?" asked Granny Webb, catching a dragonfly on her finger and holding it close to her nose.

"The *Anax junius*," she said, calling

the dragonfly by its fancy name.

Andy Shane ignored the dragonfly, even though he knew that the *Anax junius* had a bright blue tail, his favorite color. He crossed his arms and said, "I hate school."

"That can't be," said Granny Webb. "Why, Andy Shane, I loved school."

"Well, you didn't have morning meeting when you were in school," said Andy. "And you didn't have math center."

"That's true," said Granny Webb.

"*And* you didn't have Dolores Starbuckle," Andy added.

Granny Webb smiled. "No, Andy

Shane, I can't say I did."

So there, thought Andy.

Andy Shane had lived with Granny

Webb all his life. When he came

into the world, he needed someone

who could take good care of him.

Granny Webb needed someone

to share the fun of hilly woods,

salamanders, and stories. So the two of

them became a family. Just like that.

Andy Shane never longed for more.

"I hear the bus down the road, Andy Shane. Go get your lunch box," said Granny Webb.

Andy Shane didn't move.

"Don't be stubborn, Andy. You have to go to school. You know that."

There was only one person in the world more stubborn than Andy Shane, and that was Granny Webb.

Granny stood up straight.

She put her shoulders back.

She stared at Andy Shane.

She didn't move a muscle.

She didn't blink an eyelash.

She just waited.

"Oh, fine. I'm going," said Andy Shane.

That Granny Webb Stare worked every time.

The bus pulled up, and Andy Shane stepped on. He chose an empty seat and looked out the window at Granny Webb. She looked like she had just stepped on a pricker. Andy thought he must look the same way, too.

3
Granny's Surprise

Andy had no sooner hung up

his sweatshirt in his cubby when

he heard a familiar voice. It was

a voice that Andy Shane would

know anywhere.

It was the voice of his Granny
Webb.

"It's a monarch caterpillar,"
said Granny to the kids who had
gathered around her.

Andy came closer.

"Hi, Andy Shane," said Granny.
"As I was walking back to the
house, I found this caterpillar here.
I thought you and Ms. Janice
might like to keep it in the science
center."

Andy knew that their field was full of caterpillars, but he was truly happy that Granny Webb had found this one.

All the kids wanted to talk to
Granny at once.

"When will the caterpillar turn
into a butterfly?" asked Marcus.

"How long do monarch butterflies
live?" asked Jordan.

"Monarchs migrate all the way to Mexico," said Samantha.

"I like your pockets, Granny Webb," said Polly.

"Ms. Janice, *my* mother told me that visitors can't come to school until October," said Dolores Starbuckle.

"Why don't you join us anyway, Granny Webb," said Ms. Janice. "We're about to have morning meeting."

Morning meeting? Already?
Andy Shane felt like he'd *swallowed*
a caterpillar.

Ms. Janice asked the class to think
of action words — words that told
about *doing* something.

Dolores Starbuckle raised her
hand.

"Yes, Dolores," said Ms. Janice.
"Do you know an action word?"

Dolores stood up and took the
pointer from the board.

"Class, today I will teach you about *verbs*. Verbs are action words," said Dolores. "*Write* is a verb; *read* is a verb, and so is *learn*. Do any of you know an action word?"

No one raised a hand.

Dolores looked at Andy Shane.

"Andy Shane, do you know an action word?"

Andy Shane slunk down on the rug.

"Thank you, Dolores," said Ms. Janice, but Dolores didn't sit down.

"Dolores!" said Ms. Janice. But Dolores had forgotten all about Ms. Janice. She tapped her foot, waiting for Andy to answer.

"I like action words," said Granny Webb. "And I recollect a song with lots of them." Granny stood up and sang, "A mermaid splashed with the fishies in a bay."

Everyone looked at Granny.

"She flipped her tail, and a whale said, 'Hey!'" sang Granny.

"DOES ANYONE KNOW A VERB?" shouted Dolores.

No one was listening. They were

all watching Granny Webb dance

around the room.

"I SAID —"

Before Dolores could finish her sentence, everyone, even Ms. Janice, began flipping and flopping, twisting and twirling, wiggling and jiggling, and squiggling and giggling.

Everyone, that is, except for Dolores Starbuckle. She was still holding her pointer and gritting her teeth.

4

Beware the Stare

"Come on, Andy," said Granny after morning meeting. "Let's work in the math center."

"It's not our turn," whispered Andy Shane. But before he could stop her, Granny was in the math center and she had pulled out all the pizza puzzle pieces.

"You're not supposed to mix the pizzas," warned Dolores, coming into the math center. "You're not supposed to put the pepperoni with the peppers."

Granny Webb kept making mixed-up pizzas. "I like my pizzas with the works — don't you, Andy Shane?"

Andy Shane stepped back. He knew what was coming.

"MS. JANICE!" yelled Dolores Starbuckle. "SOMEONE IN THE MATH CENTER IS MISUSING THE MATERIALS!"

Andy hoped that Ms. Janice wouldn't hear Dolores, but she heard all right. She came over to the math center to see what was going on.

"Dolores," said Ms. Janice, "Granny Webb isn't misusing the materials; she's using them in a new way."

Dolores Starbuckle's face turned the color of a fire ant. She swept the pizza pieces onto the floor and stomped out of the math center.

Andy and Granny Webb decided to see how the caterpillar liked his new home in the science center. Dolores Starbuckle wandered over, too.

"I'll be the teacher," said Dolores, pointing to a picture on the wall. "What is this, Granny Webb?"

"I believe that that is a *Musca domestica*, Dolores," said Granny.

"Wrong," said Dolores. "This is a picture of a housefly."

"And what is this?" asked Dolores.

"That is a *Photinus pyralis*," said Granny Webb.

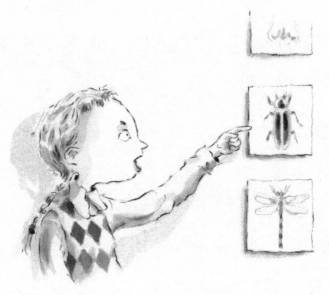

"Wrong again!" shouted Dolores. "That is a firefly. Everyone knows that."

"And what is this?" Dolores

pointed to a dragonfly.

Granny Webb didn't say anything.

"What is *this*?" repeated Dolores.

"I'm *waiting*!"

"That is an *Anax junius*," said Andy Shane. "My Granny Webb taught me all the fancy names for bugs, and she knows them better than anyone."

"OH YEAH?" said Dolores.

"Yeah," he said.

And then Andy Shane did something he'd never done before.

He gave Dolores Starbuckle the Granny Webb Stare.

He stood up straight.

He put his shoulders back.

He stared at Dolores Starbuckle.

He didn't move a muscle.

He didn't blink an eyelash.

He just waited.

Finally he asked, "What is this bug, Dolores Starbuckle?"

"Fine," she said. "It's an *Anax junius.*"

The Granny Webb Stare worked every time.

"I just remembered that my apples need picking," said Granny Webb. "I'm sorry, Andy Shane. I have to go."

"That's okay," said Andy, smiling.

"Andy Shane, will you teach me the fancy names of these bugs?" Dolores asked.

Andy Shane thought for a

moment.

"*Please?*" asked Dolores.

"All right," said Andy.

Andy told Dolores the fancy name for monarch caterpillar. He told her that soon the caterpillar would build a case called a chrysalis, which was a lot like a cocoon.

"A COCOON?" asked Dolores.

Andy stepped back.

"That rhymes with *cartoon*!" said Dolores with a laugh.

"And *lagoon*!" said Andy Shane. He laughed, too.

"And *baboon*!" said Dolores.

Maybe school isn't so bad, Andy thought. *And maybe, just maybe, Dolores and I can share our rhymes at tomorrow's morning meeting.*

ANDY
SHANE
and the
Pumpkin Trick

CONTENTS

1
Trapped

"So, Andy Shane," said Granny
Webb, "which pumpkin shall we
choose for our jack-o'-lantern
this year?"

Andy stepped back to take a good look at the pumpkins he and Granny had grown. Should he pick a big, fat, round pumpkin? Or a tall, skinny pumpkin? They all seemed to say, "Pick me! Pick me!"

"Helloooooo there!" shouted a voice.

Granny Webb and Andy Shane looked up.

Dolores Starbuckle was walking down the path, waving a white envelope in her hand.

Andy dived onto his belly between rows of pumpkins.

Granny laughed. "Too late, Andy Shane. You've definitely been spotted."

"Andy Shane," called Dolores as she approached, "you forgot your invitation at school."

Dolores's birthday was in two days. So was Halloween.

"I wouldn't want you to forget my party," said Dolores. "And I know that you'll need time to think about my present."

"Oh, we wouldn't have forgotten," said Granny Webb. "I promised your mother I would help out this year."

Andy looked up at Granny Webb. How could she? Now he was really trapped into going.

"Wow!" exclaimed Dolores. "Did you and Granny grow all these pumpkins, Andy Shane?"

"Yup," Andy said. "We sure did!"

"You're lucky," said Dolores. "We bought a pumpkin at Glories of Nature, but someone came along and smashed it last night."

"Someone smashed your pumpkin?" asked Andy. "Why would they do that?"

Granny Webb shook her head. "Such a waste. Come inside, Dolores, and help us make pumpkin muffins for your birthday. Then you can tell us all about those tricksters."

The minute Dolores entered Andy's house, she began poking around. She picked up a jar of marbles from the kitchen counter.

"Whose are these?" she asked.

"Mine," said Andy.

"I like the big marble at the bottom. Ooooh, and look at this sparkly one here!" said Dolores. "Will you play marbles with me sometime?"

Andy didn't know what to say.

"Tell us more about the tricksters," said Granny, mixing up the muffin batter.

"As soon as it got dark, they smashed all the pumpkins on our street," said Dolores.

"Did anyone catch them?" asked Andy.

"Nope," said Dolores. "No one heard them."

"We'll have to give you another pumpkin, then," said Granny Webb.

When they returned to the
pumpkin patch, Dolores charged
over to the biggest, fattest one.

"Isn't this the best pumpkin?"
said Dolores as she picked it from
the vine.

It *did* seem to be the best one. But then Andy noticed a rounder, jollier pumpkin, and another that was more orange than the rest. *They're* ALL *the best,* he thought.

"Great," said Granny Webb. "As soon as the muffins are done, I'll drive you and your pumpkin home."

"Can Andy come, too?"

"Sure," said Granny Webb.

"He can stay and help me get ready for my party," said Dolores.

"Get ready for your party?" said

Andy. "It's two days away!"

"It's never too early to prepare for

a social event," noted Dolores.

2
Party Plans

Dolores carried the pumpkin

from Granny's truck to her front

porch. She put it on the left side

of the steps.

"We need to find its best side,"

Dolores said.

She turned the pumpkin around

and around.

"Perfect!" she said finally. "Let's get ready for the party!"

Andy made a face. He was definitely not showing *his* best side.

First they filled a big tub with

water for apple dunking.

Next they hung strings from
the rafters in the living room —
strings that would hold powdered
doughnuts.

Then they began blowing up
balloons.

When Andy had blown

up thirteen balloons,

he got an idea.

"Let's set a trap!" he said.

"Don't be silly. What would

we need a trap for?"

asked Dolores.

"To trap the tricksters!"

exclaimed Andy. "I bet they'll

come back for your new pumpkin."

"They will?" asked Dolores.

"It's the best," said Andy. "You said it yourself."

Dolores thought for a moment. "I suppose we should figure out a trap," she said, picking up her clipboard and pen. 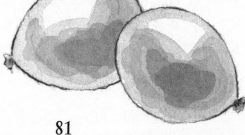 "It's always good to plan ahead."

Andy couldn't believe his luck. Catching the tricksters was *his* idea of fun.

"Let's build a cage and hang it out an upstairs window," he said. "Then when the tricksters come up the steps . . ."

Dolores stopped writing.

"We don't have any metal to build

a cage with," she said.

Oh, thought Andy. *True enough.*

"We can dig a big hole," he said, "and cover it with sticks and leaves and grass and stuff. When the pumpkin smashers walk across the top, they'll fall in the pit and —"

"My father would *never* let us dig a hole in the yard," said Dolores. She crossed out the second idea.

"We can hang a bucket of water from a string," said Andy. "And when the tricksters are directly underneath —"

"How do you know that the tricksters will go *directly* underneath?" asked Dolores.

"All right, then," he said. "*You* think of an idea!"

"We'll be ghosts!" announced Dolores.

"Ghosts?" said Andy.

"Ghosts. And when the tricksters come up on the porch to steal the pumpkin, we'll rush out and scare them."

"No trap?" asked Andy.

"It *is* a trap," said Dolores. "It's just a different *kind* of trap."

Andy wasn't sure about her plan. But he didn't have a better one.

Andy and Dolores went to search

for sheets.

"You can wear this," said Dolores.

"It has flowers on it!" said Andy.

"My mom doesn't have any plain white sheets," said Dolores. "We can be the ghosts of the gardens — ghosts that scare anyone who messes with the glories of nature!"

"Oh, brother!" said Andy.

3
Not-So-Glorious Ghosts

Andy and Dolores huddled under the porch. It seemed as if they had been down there forever, waiting for it to get dark. Andy pulled a marble out of his pocket.

"Wow!" whispered Dolores. "I've never seen one that glows."

"This is my lucky marble," said Andy.

"May I hold it?" Dolores asked.

Just then Andy and Dolores heard

footsteps coming up the walkway.

Dolores peeked out from under the

steps and gave Andy the thumbs-up.

They pulled the sheets over their

heads.

"Ooooooh," Dolores moaned.

Andy followed her out from under
the porch.

"Ooooooh," he groaned.

"What's that?" said one of the tricksters.

"OOOOOOH!" Dolores yelled.

Andy couldn't see where he was going. He tripped on the hem of his sheet and fell face-down.

The tricksters doubled over laughing.

"Ooh, what scary ghosts!" one of them said.

Then they grabbed the pumpkin, smashed it on the ground, and took off running.

"Stop messing with our pumpkins!" Dolores shouted. "They're glories of nature!"

Andy untangled himself from his sheet.

What a stupid idea this was, he thought.

Then he saw Dolores kneeling over her smashed pumpkin. She was crying.

"Two pumpkins in two days," she sniffed.

That evening, Andy Shane pushed his meatballs from one side of his plate to the other.

"You look like I served you porcupine stew instead of your favorite supper," said Granny Webb.

"I still need to think of a present for Dolores," said Andy, carrying his plate over to the sink.

"Whoops!" he said.

Marbles bounced all over the kitchen floor.

Andy took a step and stumbled on a marble. And then another. His arms flailed in the air, but he couldn't keep his balance. He slip-slid to the floor.

"Aaugh!" he said. "This has been the worst day ever!"

"Have a nice *trip*? See you next *fall*!" Granny said, laughing. She was like that, always turning tragedy into fun.

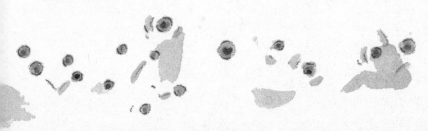

Andy had to laugh, too. Then he started to collect all the marbles that had rolled from the kitchen counter to the front door.

That's when he got a great idea.

4
Tricking the Tricksters

Granny Webb carried the muffins while Andy Shane carried the roundest pumpkin to Dolores Starbuckle's front door.

"Why, a spider and a fly have arrived!" Mrs. Starbuckle said.

"We're a *Grammostola rosea* and a *Musca domestica*," said Granny Webb. She knew all the fancy names for bugs.

"Is that my present?" Dolores asked Andy.

Andy turned pink. "It's part of it," he said. "You have to wait for the rest."

"Come dunk for apples, then," said Dolores.

Andy followed Dolores to the tub

for apple dunking and to the strings

for doughnut munching.

Then Dolores took Andy to the haunted room to put his hands in a bowl full of eyeballs.

"Ugh," said Peter and Mindy.

"Mmmm," said Andy Shane, "*crunchy!*"

"How did you know they were grapes?" asked Dolores Starbuckle.

Andy just smiled. He didn't tell her that Granny Webb had played that trick on him last Halloween.

When the party was over, Andy
Shane and Granny Webb stayed to
help clean up.

Suddenly they heard a noise on
the porch.

"Shh!" said Andy. "It's the

tricksters."

"Well, I'm not going to let them

get my pumpkin again," said

Dolores.

"No, wait!" Andy said. "Watch."

Granny Webb came into the room and joined Andy and Dolores at the window. Andy felt like a soda-pop can that was about to burst.

One of the tricksters looked up and saw the three of them peering out. He grabbed the pumpkin and turned to run.

At that moment, the bottom of the pumpkin fell out.

Hundreds of marbles rolled down the porch steps.

Bimmety, Bimmety, Bim

BAM

Bim, BAM

Bim, bam

"Aaugh! Let's get out of here!" the

tricksters shouted.

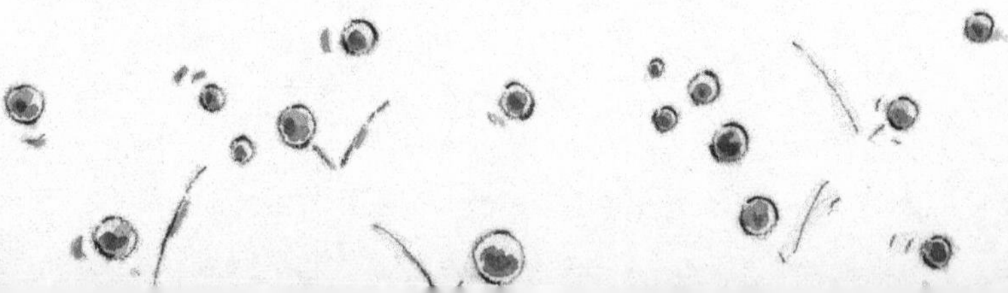

"Andy Shane, you tricked the tricksters!" exclaimed Dolores.

She scooped the marbles into a plastic bag and handed it to him.

Andy smiled. He gave the bag back to Dolores.

"Happy birthday!" he said. "This is the second part of your present."

"Really?" said Dolores. "They're all for me?"

"Yup," said Andy. "That's half of my collection. I kept the other half so we could play marbles together."

"You'll play marbles with me?"

asked Dolores.

Andy nodded.

"Tomorrow?"

"Sure," said Andy.

"This has turned out to be a great

Halloween," Dolores said, "and a

great birthday!"

Andy Shane had to agree.

For my Uncle Bob — Let me entertain you
J. R. J.

To Carter and Samantha
A. C.

ANDY
SHANE
and the
Queen of Egypt

CONTENTS

1
I Am the Queen

Andy Shane parked his bike and

shifted the weight in his backpack.

"Let's meet by the *tree* when the

clock says *three*," he said.

"I will ride my *bike*, or we will have to *hike*," said Granny Webb.

Granny and Andy had been talking in rhymes all morning. It was hard to stop once you got started.

"Oh, wait!" said Granny.

"Don't be *late,*" said Andy, waving

good-bye.

"No, really," called Granny Webb.

"I have something for you."

Andy turned back to see what
Granny was pulling from her pocket.
Whatever it was appeared to be on
the end of a long gold chain.

"Oooh," said Andy, moving
closer. It was a dark green bug
frozen in clear plastic. "A beetle!"

"A scarab beetle!" said Granny.

"Is this Egyptian?" asked Andy.

Andy knew that the scarab beetle was important to the people of ancient Egypt.

"I think so," said Granny Webb, handing it to Andy. "I knew you were thinking about African countries last night, and a memory of it popped into my *head* while I was heading off to *bed*!"

Andy laughed at Granny's rhyme. "Thanks," he said, and he headed into school.

"What do you think of my new sandals, Andy Shane?" asked Dolores Starbuckle as they sat down at their desks.

"Cool," said Andy.

"I made them myself with milk cartons and glitter," said Dolores.

Andy noticed that Dolores Starbuckle was particularly fancy this morning.

"I hope each of you has chosen an African country," said Ms. Janice. "We need to get ready for the school Culture Fair."

Dolores Starbuckle sat up as tall as she could.

"Polly," said Ms. Janice with her pen in the air, ready to write, "what country would you like to learn about?"

"Kenya," said Polly. "My uncle went to Kenya."

Kenya was a large country with deserts and rain forests. Andy had *almost* chosen Kenya.

"Ahmed?" asked Ms. Janice.

"The Gambia."

Ms. Janice told the class that The Gambia was a small farming country. Andy thought he might like to be a farmer one day.

"Andy Shane?"

Andy touched his pocket. "Egypt," he said softly.

"I'm sorry, Andy," said Ms. Janice. "I didn't hear you."

"I think he said Ethiopia," said Dolores. She was always trying to be helpful.

"Is that right, Andy?" asked Ms. Janice.

Andy shook his head.

"Do you mean Nigeria, Andy Shane?" said Dolores. "I think you mean Ni-*geeeeee*-ria."

"Egypt," Andy said more loudly.

"But you can't choose Egypt," said Dolores, springing out of her seat. "I'm wearing my white Egyptian clothes and my gold jewelry. I even made sandals. I am the QUEEN of Egypt."

The class laughed.

Andy slumped down on his desk.

Why did Dolores Starbuckle always

insist on getting what *she* wanted?

But he couldn't argue with her —

not in front of the whole class!

Andy knew everyone was waiting for his answer. He wished he could disappear altogether.

"We'll work this out later," said Ms. Janice. She finished calling on the children. Then she told the class to line up for a visit to the library, where they could begin their research. "Andy Shane," she said, "you're line leader."

Dolores stood in front of Andy.

"Andy Shane, you know I *loooove* Egypt!" she said. "I even have a model of a sphinx!"

"What's a sphinx?" asked Polly.

"A statue. Mine has a lion's body with a bird's head," said Dolores.

"Weird," said Polly.

"But I have this," said Andy.

He pulled out the beetle.

"Oooh," said Dolores, admiring the necklace. She sighed a long, deep sigh. Then her face brightened. "Can we work together, Andy Shane?"

Andy didn't know what to say. He liked to take his time with ideas, see how they felt. And right now, he did not feel like giving Dolores her way. "I'll think about it," he said.

2
Pineapple Pyramids

That night, like every Tuesday night
when her father and mother went to
choir practice, Dolores ate dinner
with Andy Shane and Granny Webb.

Andy was on the kitchen floor coloring a picture of a sphinx when Dolores arrived.

"I wish I could draw like you," said Dolores.

Andy looked up to say thanks, but Dolores was already busy tying on her favorite Granny Webb apron — the one with the big pockets. She hopped up on the stool near the counter.

Granny Webb was emptying chunks of pineapple from a can into a bowl.

"I'll do that, Granny Webb," said

Dolores. "I like to be helpful."

Granny Webb smiled and handed

Dolores the can.

"Wow!" said Dolores. "I never noticed that before."

Andy wanted to say, "Noticed what?" But Dolores went right on talking.

"May I serve the pineapple pizza tonight? *Please?*" asked Dolores.

"Well, it's Andy's turn to set the table, but I'm sure he wouldn't mind some help. Isn't that right, Andy?"

"Sure," said Andy.

After Granny took the pizza from the oven and let it cool, Dolores carefully arranged slices on each plate. Then she stood back and admired her work.

"My, my, my," said Granny Webb.

Andy came over to see what the fuss was about. "What *is* this?" he asked.

"Why, Andy," said Granny, "it's pineapple pizza. One of your favorites."

"But how come the pineapple is all piled up on the side of the plate?" asked Andy.

"Don't you see?" said Dolores. "The pineapple chunks are little bricks. I made you a pineapple pyramid!"

"But how come the pizza has bald spots?" said Andy, pointing to his plate. "The pizza and the pineapple are supposed to be together!"

"Think about it, Andy Shane," said Dolores. "The most popular booths at the Culture Fair always have food samples. If we work together on the project, I can make lots and lots of pineapple pyramids! We'll be a huge hit!"

"Oh, brother," said Andy.

Andy knew that Dolores was looking at him while he ate, hoping he'd cave in and say they could work together. But the only thing that caved in that night was his pineapple pyramid.

3
Walk Like an Egyptian

When Andy walked into his classroom the next day, he noticed two
things. Number one, Ms. Janice's
big yellow bag with orange flowers
on it was not beside her desk.

And number two, in the center of Ms. Janice's desk was a giant stack of paper. This could mean only one thing.

Andy Shane looked at Dolores.

Dolores Starbuckle nodded.

They were having a substitute teacher.

Sure enough, a tall man came into the room, explained that Ms. Janice was not feeling well, and handed out work sheets.

Andy finished all the math problems on the page. Then he began drawing pictures of baseballs and baseball bats all around the edge of his paper. According to Andy Shane, today was the best day of the year. It was the first day of T-ball!

Dolores cleared her throat.

Andy looked up to see what she was doing.

She was writing their names in Egyptian hieroglyphs.

Andy pretended he didn't see.

The tall man handed out a second set of work sheets, and then a third. When Dolores had finished her third paper, she asked the substitute teacher if they could make get-well cards for Ms. Janice.

"A wonderful suggestion!" said the substitute.

Andy Shane reached into his desk to find his crayons. He pulled out his action figure of Giraffe Man.

"Hey!" he cried. His Giraffe Man was wrapped up in toilet paper.

"Doesn't he make a great mummy?" asked Dolores.

"Ugh!" said Andy. After he finished his card, he would draw a sign for his desk that read *No Trespassing*.

That evening, Andy's coach asked Andy to play right field. In T-ball, you have to have a strong arm to play right field.

Andy Shane looked at the bleachers to locate Granny Webb. Sitting next to Granny was Dolores Starbuckle. Andy Shane couldn't help noticing that she was *still* wearing her fancy Egyptian clothes.

Both teams had batters that had
no trouble hitting the ball off the tee.
By the final inning, the score was
tied. A girl known as Slugger was up
next. Andy adjusted his cap and
backed up. He would be ready.

Suddenly, music blared from the
stands. Dolores was standing on
the top bleacher. Only she wasn't just
standing. She was dancing. She was
dancing to a song called "Walk Like
an Egyptian."

Andy knew that Dolores loved this song. She loved showing others how she could walk like an Egyptian along with the music. She strutted and turned, strutted and turned.

People in the stands applauded.

But Slugger wasn't watching
Dolores. She got into position,
pulled back the bat, and popped
that ball into right field.

"Catch it, Andy!" yelled Granny Webb.

But Andy didn't catch it. He was too busy watching Dolores. So were the other kids in the outfield.

The ball rolled past Andy and hit

the back fence.

Slugger scored a home run, and her team won the game.

Andy Shane would not even look at Dolores when he came off the field.

At that moment, she was not the queen of anything.

4
A Team

That night Andy couldn't get to sleep.

First, he couldn't believe he had

missed the ball and lost the game.

Second, he knew that tomorrow he had to stand up and tell the class his plans for the Culture Fair. Whenever Andy had to speak to the whole class, he felt as if his throat took a dive and hid somewhere deep in his stomach.

"Here's a 'sorry' note," said Dolores as Andy walked through the classroom door. It was in Egyptian hieroglyphs.

"Do you want me to read it to you?" asked Dolores.

"No," Andy said. He didn't even

try to read it. He just stuffed it into

his pocket.

Later, when the class was painting an enormous map of the continent of Africa, Dolores handed Andy the paintbrush with the blue handle. Everyone in Ms. Janice's class knew that the brush with the blue handle was the biggest and the best of all.

"No, thanks," said Andy. He didn't even look at Dolores when he spoke.

When the painting was finished, Ms. Janice asked each student to come to the front of the room and give a report on his or her Culture Day plans.

Peter went first. He showed the class pictures of masks from Mali. "I'm going to make a mask," he said.

Polly showed the class a mobile she was working on. Hanging from the mobile were pictures of the desert, the forest, the seashore, and a big city. All of these places were in Kenya.

"Andy, show us what you've done," said Ms. Janice.

Andy walked to the front of the room. He began to speak but realized he had nothing in his hands. Peter had shown something. Polly had shown something. What should he do?

"I want —" Andy paused. "I want . . ."

"Your mummy!" said Dolores.

Everyone laughed.

Dolores reached into Andy's
desk and took out Giraffe Man.
She handed him to Andy.

"Oooh," the students said.

Andy Shane held the mummy
action figure but still looked as if
he didn't know what to say.

Dolores waved her hands from the

back of the room to get

his attention.

She made

her hands go

around her neck,

like a necklace.

"I have a necklace," said Andy, "that

has a scarab beetle on it. People in

ancient Egypt believed that the

scarab-beetle god pushed the sun

across the sky. And . . ."

"Yes, Andy?" said Ms. Janice.

Dolores made her hands and face look like the sphinx that Andy had drawn at home.

"Oh, I made a picture of a sphinx," said Andy.

"You should see Andy's picture, Ms. Janice," said Dolores. "It came out really well!"

Andy could feel his face getting warmer, but he was happy. He took a big breath and sat down.

"Thank you, Andy," said Ms. Janice. "Dolores, why don't you come up and tell us about the country you've chosen."

Dolores walked to the front of the room.

She pointed to the map the children
had painted and said, "I've chosen the
teeny tiny country of Togo, which is —"
"No!" shouted Andy.

All eyes turned to him.

"Andy?" said Ms. Janice.

Andy stood up. "Dolores and I are going to work together — on Egypt."

"Really?" asked Dolores.

Andy nodded.

"Oh, thank you, thank you, thank you, Andy Shane!"

For a minute, Andy was afraid Dolores was going to hug him. Or she was going to strut back and forth doing her Egyptian dance. Instead,

she simply wiggled her toes in her

Egyptian sandals and smiled.

"Wonderful," said Ms. Janice.

Andy smiled back. There was no
doubt about it. He and Dolores
Starbuckle, the Queen of Egypt,
would make a great team.

ANDY
SHANE
Is NOT in Love

CONTENTS

1
New Girl in Town

Dolores Starbuckle leaned over Andy Shane's desk. She pointed to the picture Andy was drawing. "Make a turret here," she said.

"What's a turret?" asked Yumi.

"It's the pointy part of a castle," said Dolores.

"Who said we're making a castle?" asked Andy. He and Dolores were busy planning the snow fort they would make when the snow was warm enough and wet enough to stick.

"Good morning, class," said Ms. Janice.

"Good morning, Ms. Janice," said the students, looking up from their books and games and papers.

Ms. Janice was not alone. She had her arm around a girl who was wearing pink overalls and lime-green sneakers tied with ribbons instead of shoelaces. The girl's eyes seemed to dance.

"This is Lark Alice Bell," said Ms. Janice. "She's just moved to town and will be in our class this year."

"Hello, Lark," said Dolores, shooting her hand into the air. "I'll be your helper if you want. I know all the class rules and procedures, such as, 'Be responsible and respectful.'"

"Thank you, Dolores," said Ms. Janice. "Perhaps you can be Lark's guide on the playground. I thought Andy Shane might like to help Lark in class this morning."

"Lucky duck," whispered Dolores.

"Andy, please come forward and meet Lark," said Ms. Janice.

Andy's face turned the color of his favorite crayon: Razzle Dazzle Rose.

"Oooh," said the other kids.

Andy showed Lark where to sit

during morning meeting,

where to find the math materials,

and where to sharpen her pencil.

At recess, Dolores made it clear

that it was *her* turn to be the helper.

So Andy ran off to climb the big

snowbank left by the plow.

He dug a hole and sat in the bottom.

It was a peaceful place to be.

"Hi, Andy Shane," said a voice from the top of his hole. "What are you *doing* in there?"

"Just sitting," said Andy. "Come on down."

Lark slipped in next to Andy. "This is like a cave," she said.

Andy smiled. He was proud of his hole.

"The closet in my old house felt like a cave," said Lark. "That's where my dog had her puppies."

"You have puppies?" asked Andy.

"Four," said Lark. "They're yellow Lab puppies. They're so cute. They have these little bodies with giant paws and big noses."

"I have wanted a dog my whole life," said Andy. "My Granny Webb said *maybe* I was old enough to get one."

"Does 'maybe' mean yes, or does 'maybe' mean no?"

"With Granny Webb, 'maybe' means 'maybe,'" said Andy.

"*Maybe*," said Lark, "you can have one of mine."

2
First Comes Love

"There you are, Lark!" said Dolores,
peering down the hole. "I've been
looking everywhere for you! The bell
already rang!"

"It did? Oh, no!" said Andy. "We have to go!"

Lark and Andy squirmed up out of the snow cave and ran as fast as they could. They reached the end of the line just as the last of the children were entering the building.

"Hurry up, Andy! Hurry up, Lark!"

called Dolores from inside the door.

Big kids were standing in the hall waiting for their turn at the water fountain. One started singing, "Andy and Lark sitting in a tree, K-I-S-S-I-N-G!"

Andy Shane stopped. He put his shoulders back. He stared at those kids. He didn't move a muscle.

One boy laughed nervously.

"Come on, Lark," said Andy.

"You are not being responsible and
respectful!" Dolores told the big kids.

Without even taking her snowsuit off, Dolores marched right over to Andy's desk. "For your information, *I* was supposed to be Lark's helper at recess."

But Andy wasn't ready to listen. He was writing down his name and phone number for Lark. Lark wrote down her name and phone number for Andy.

"Do you want *my* phone number?" Dolores asked Lark, but Lark just looked confused.

"Today you will need a reading
buddy," said Ms. Janice.

Lark reached out and grabbed
Andy's hand.

That startled Andy. He and Dolores

had always been reading buddies. But

Andy was supposed to be Lark's helper.

He looked at Dolores and shrugged.

Dolores just turned and walked away.

While Ms. Janice reminded them of the jobs of reading buddies, Andy Shane doodled on the back of his notebook. He made a big heart and wrote LAB inside.

Dolores, who was supposed to be reading with Polly, leaned way over in her seat to see what Andy was writing.

Andy tried to cover it with his hand, but Dolores had already seen.

"L-A-B," she whispered loudly.

"That stands for *Lark Alice Bell.* Why, you *are* in love, Andy Shane!"

Then she fell out of her seat onto the floor.

3

Hurt Feelings

On Saturday, Lark came to Andy's
house.

"Why, Lark, I've heard so much
about you," said Granny Webb.

She made them cocoa with marsh-mallows. "Now tell me about the puppies."

Lark told Granny that all of the puppies had been spoken for except one. "He is the most playful puppy of all," said Lark. "If you give him a carrot top, he'll chase it across the floor like it's a bug or a mouse."

"I guess we'd better start saving our carrot tops," said Granny.

Andy jumped up and wrapped his arms around Granny. "You'll see, Granny. I'll take really good care of this puppy."

"We'll have to think of a name," said Granny Webb.

When they finished their cocoa, Andy and Lark put on their winter gear and headed outside.

"This is the field behind my house," said Andy.

"Dogs love to run in fields," said Lark.

"And these are my woods," said Andy.

"Dogs love to sniff in woods," said Lark.

"And this is my sledding hill," said Andy.

"*I* love to sled!" said Lark.

Andy got his flying saucer, and he and Lark slid down the hill over and over again.

"Hey," said Lark, "want to build a snow fort?"

There was nothing Andy loved more in winter than building snow forts. He and Lark scooped up the perfectly sticky snow and piled it high.

Then they crawled inside. They made two little seats, a table, and a shelf.

Andy recognized that voice. That voice belonged to another person who loved to build snow forts—someone who had planned all year with Andy to make the coolest fort ever, someone who was waiting for Andy to call and say, "The snow is ready! Come now!"

"Dolores!" said Andy, jumping out

of the fort.

"I was waiting for you to call, Andy.

The snow is perfect."

"I forgot, but look," he said, stepping back and pointing to his fort. "Isn't it cool?"

"Wow! It *is* cool. Did you do this all by yourself?" asked Dolores.

Two snowflake mittens appeared from the fort. Lark popped out.

Andy felt terrible. He hadn't meant to build a fort without Dolores. And now it looked as if he'd had a fort party and she wasn't invited.

"Want to help us put the roof on?" asked Andy.

"I thought you were my best friend, Andy Shane," said Dolores, crossing her arms over her chest. "I can't believe you and Lark built this fort without me! That is so mean!"

Dolores turned and stomped back
to the driveway. She nearly bumped
into Granny Webb, who was carrying
a soup pot.

"What's the matter, Dolores?"

asked Granny.

"She's mad because *we* were

supposed to make a fort today," said

Andy, running over.

"Oh, I see," said Granny. She reached down and took Dolores's hand. "I think it's time we all met Andy's new best friend," she said.

4
Things Are Not Always as They Seem

"I am not in the mood for any more new friends," said Dolores as Lark led the way up the hill to her new house.

"Especially when they cause your old friends to treat you shabbily."

When they arrived, Granny Webb handed Lark's mother the pot of soup. "Welcome to the neighborhood," she said.

Lark's mother started telling Granny all about the move. She seemed really happy to have a new friend.

Lark led Dolores and Andy downstairs to the basement.

"You know, I did have plans of my own this afternoon," said Dolores.

"I don't need to be following you around.

I am sure there are lots of people who
would like to be my friend."

"Dolores, you've got it all wrong,"
said Andy.

Dolores's voice just got louder.
"People who wouldn't desert me on
the playground. People who would be
my reading buddy. People who would
like to build a snow fort with me."

Lark brought them to a large box.

"Oooh," said Dolores, reaching in.

"Puppies!"

"Which one is mine?"

asked Andy.

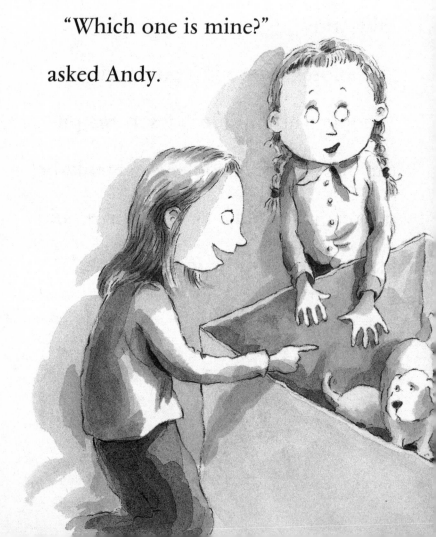

Lark pointed to the one trying to climb the sides of the box. Every time he stretched, he flipped over. "That one," she said, laughing.

"Yours?" asked Dolores.

"Yup," said Andy, picking up the pup and holding him to his cheek. "Granny said I could have one."

"You lucky duck!" said Dolores, patting the puppy in Andy's arms. "What kind of dog is he?"

"He's a Lab," said Lark.

"A Lab?" said Dolores. "L-A-B?

Oh!" Now her face was the color of

Razzle Dazzle Rose.

"Granny Webb was right," said

Dolores. "You do have a new best

friend, Andy."

Lark sighed. "I miss *my* best friends," she said.

"But you have us!" said Dolores, putting her arm around Lark. "Andy and I will be your new best friends."

"And Lucky Duck, too!" said

Andy, holding up his puppy.

"You can't call a dog a duck," said

Dolores.

"I can if I want to," said Andy.

"Right, Lucky Duck?" He gave his

dog a big squeeze. Lucky Duck licked

Andy's face.

"Andy Shane's in love," said Dolores.

But this time, no one seemed to mind.

Andy Shane and the Pumpkin Trick
Library of Congress Catalog Card Number 2004062872
ISBN 978-0-7636-2605-1 (hardcover)
ISBN 978-0-7636-3306-6 (paperback)

Andy Shane and the Queen of Egypt
Library of Congress Catalog Card Number 2007032003
ISBN 978-0-7636-3211-3 (hardcover)
ISBN 978-0-7636-4404-8 (paperback)

Andy Shane Is NOT in Love
Library of Congress Catalog Card Number 2007052880
ISBN 978-0-7636-3212-0 (hardcover)
ISBN 978-0-7636-4403-1 (paperback)

ISBN 978-1-5362-0046-1 (paperback collection)

18 19 20 21 22 23 BVG 10 9 8 7 6 5 4 3 2 1

Printed in Berryville, VA, U.S.A.

This book was typeset in Vendome.
The illustrations were done in black pencil and black watercolor wash.

Candlewick Press
99 Dover Street
Somerville, Massachusetts 02144

visit us at www.candlewick.com

Check out Andy and Dolores's adventures!

#1 ***Andy Shane and the Very Bossy Dolores Starbuckle***

#2 ***Andy Shane and the Pumpkin Trick***

#3 ***Andy Shane and the Queen of Egypt***

#4 ***Andy Shane Is NOT in Love***

#5 ***Andy Shane and the Barn Sale Mystery***

#6 ***Andy Shane, Hero at Last***

Jennifer Richard Jacobson

illustrated by Abby Carter

www.candlewick.com

Jennifer Richard Jacobson has written many books for young children, including all of the Andy Shane titles. "There is a little bit of Andy Shane in me," she says. "I remember what it was like to be bullied in school. But I also remember tattling, so I guess I have a bit of Dolores Starbuckle in me, too." Jennifer Richard Jacobson lives in Maine.

Abby Carter is the illustrator of many books for children, including the other books about Andy Shane. She also illustrated *My Hippie Grandmother* by Reeve Lindbergh, *Full House: An Invitation to Fractions* by Dayle Ann Dodds, and *Maggie's Monkeys* by Linda Sanders-Wells. Abby Carter lives in Maine.